CLARK THE SHARK
TAKES HEART

WRITTEN BY **BRUCE HALE**   ILLUSTRATED BY **GUY FRANCIS**

SCHOLASTIC INC.

To my sweet Janette, with moochas smooches
—B.H.

To Stacy, Jann, and Rayna
—G.F.

ISBN 978-0-545-83933-4

12 11 10 9 8 7 6 5   16 17 18 19 20/0

Printed in the U.S.A.   40

First Scholastic printing, February 2015

The artist used acrylic to create the illustrations for this book.
Typography by Sean Boggs

Of all the fish at Theodore Roosterfish Elementary, no one was stronger than Clark the Shark. He wasn't afraid of whirlpools or whales, giant squids or riptides—but one thing made him nervous.

Girls.

"If you like a girl and it's almost her birthday, what do you do?" Clark asked his best friend, Joey Mackerel.

"You give her candy, you send a card," said Joey. "Badda-bim, badda-boom—no big deal."

"But what if you REALLY *like* her?"

"Who do you like?" said Joey. "Amanda Eelwiggle?"

"No!" cried Clark.

"Letty Lungfish?"

"No way!"

"Mrs. Inkydink?"

"*Eew*," said Clark. "No, I like Anna Angelfish."

"If you want her to know it," said Joey, "you've got to show her how you feel."

All day long, Clark fretted and fussed; he worried and wondered.
What would impress Anna the most?

Then he had the biggest and best and most shark-errific idea.

"Girls like winners," Clark told Joey. "So hold on to your fin and watch me win!"

"But—" said Joey.

Coach Crabby blew his whistle. "On your marks . . . get set . . . go!"

Clark the Shark swam up a storm. He was faster than Roger, faster than Rita, faster than fast!

But when Clark turned to see if Anna was watching, he wasn't fast enough to miss the reef.

Woosha-whappa . . .

YOWCH!

"Big and flashy isn't always best," said Joey.
"I'll do better tomorrow," said Clark.

The next day, the school boat passed Clark and Joey on the way to school. There sat Anna, sweet as jellyfish pie. But a blue whale's wake sent the school boat spinning!

Woosha-walla...

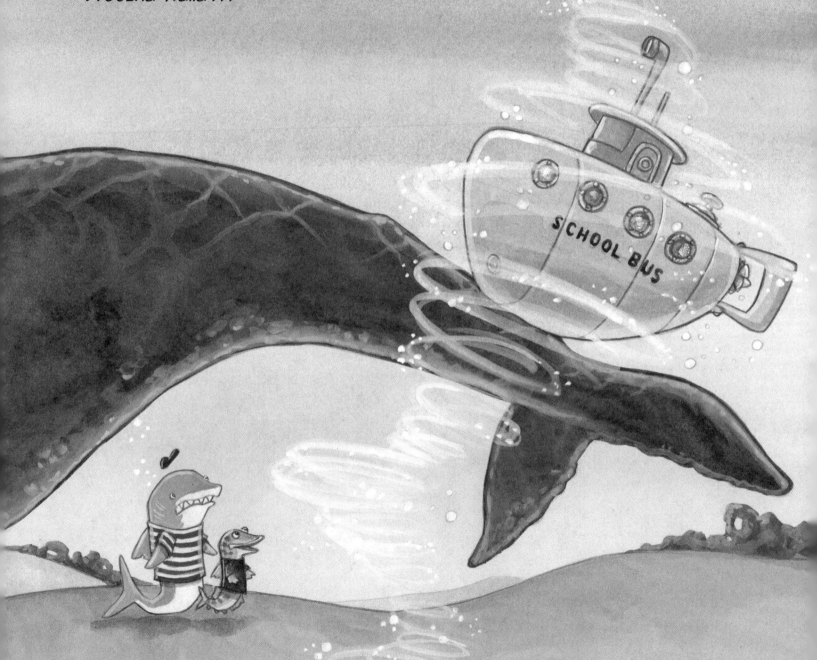

CRUNCH! It wedged between two rocks.

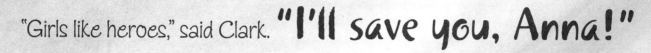

"Girls like heroes," said Clark. **"I'll save you, Anna!"**

And he swam at the bottom of the boat with all his sharky might.
"Wait—" said Joey.
Woosha-whacka . . .

WHOMP! Clark hit so hard that everyone went flying, books and bags and all!

"Big and crashy doesn't work either," said Joey.

"I'll do better tomorrow," said Clark. "Tomorrow's her birthday!"

And Anna didn't even notice.

The next day, Clark went to school extra early. "Girls like a big show," he told himself. "So I'll give her a show." With care, he spelled out **HAPPY BIRTHDAY, ANNA!** across the hall in seaweed letters ten feet tall.

Right on time, along came the school boat.
And along came Anna with a group of her friends.

But before she could spot her surprise, a school of barracuda blasted down the hall.

Woosha-washa...

SPLOOF! They swam so fast, they blew the seaweed off the coral and into the students.

"Who made this mess?" cried Anna and her friends.

"So much for big and grassy," said Joey.

At recess, Clark wouldn't play with his friends. He just moped and muttered and grumped by himself.

"Why so glum, chum?" said Joey.

"Every time I try to make a big impression, something goes wrong."
Joey shook his head. "Bigger isn't always better. Sometimes the best things—like me—come in small packages."

Later, at lunch, Clark was playing whirly-doodle. After one wild game, he spun into the sea grass and landed with a *thump*. And there in the green, he spotted something.

Clark parted the grass, and right before his eyes, he found the tiniest, pinkest, most perfectly heart-shaped shell. Clark thought of Joey's words. Could something small be best of all?

Then he carefully picked up the shell and brought it to Anna.
Woosha-washa . . .

HMM?

"Um, this is for you, Anna. Happy birthday!" Clark held his breath. Would she like his gift, or laugh in his sharky face?

Anna smiled. "Clark, that's so sweet."

"Not as sweet as you!" Clark the Shark blushed four shades of red. "I . . . like you, Anna."

"I like you too, Clark."

And that afternoon, when the school day was done, Anna didn't catch the school boat after all. Instead, she swam home with Clark the Shark.

Woosha-washa...

AWWW.